JUV/E   Fields, Julia.
PZ
8.3     The green lion of
.F458    Zion Street
Gr
1988

$13.95                    cop.2

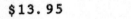

| | DATE | | |
|---|---|---|---|
| AUG | 1989 | | |
| | | | |
| | | | |
| | | | |
| | | | |
| | | | |
| | | | |
| | | | |
| | | | |
| | | | |
| | | | |

# The Green Lion
# of Zion Street

# The Green Lion of Zion Street

*Julia Fields*

*illustrated by Jerry Pinkney*

*Margaret K. McElderry Books*
NEW YORK

Margaret K. McElderry Books
Macmillan Publishing Company
866 Third Avenue
New York, NY 10022
Collier Macmillan Canada, Inc.

First Edition

Text composition by Linoprint Composition, New York, New York
Printed and bound by Toppan Printing Company in Japan

10  9  8  7  6  5  4  3  2  1

Library of Congress Cataloging-in-Publication Data

Fields, Julia.
The green lion of Zion Street/Julia Fields; illustrated by
Jerry Pinkney.—1st ed.
p.  cm.
Summary: The stone lion on Zion Street, proud and fierce, instills
fear and admiration in those who see it in the cold city fog.
ISBN 0-689-50414-4
[1. Lions—Fiction.  2. City and town life—Fiction.  3. Stories
in rhyme.]  I. Pinkney, Jerry, ill.  II. Title.
PZ8.3.F458Gr  1988      [E]—dc19
87-15519  CIP  AC

The original pictures for The Green Lion of Zion Street
are pencil and watercolor paintings.

To  Stephanie L. Fields
    Eugene Redmond
    Robert Locke
    Ronald C. Foreman
                        J.F.


For the Star of Bethlehem Baptist Church
              Drama Committee
                        J.P..

Sometime
  the bus be's late
  and you have to stand
  in the streets and wait
  in weather ten times colder
  than a roller skate.

Everybody standing at the stop
by the bubble light,
and the whole white morning look
just like night
'cause that fog jump the bridge
like a big gray hog, and it get so thick
you can hardly see the park—
and this—this when it not even time—
even nigh time—for to get dark.
And somebody always walking there.
Singing. Melting out quick
like some sly shark.
                    Singing.

They singing 'cause they scared.
Out real loud!
But if you just whisper, "Boo!…"
they will burn that foggy bottom
            dry.
Whoever it is will fly
like a space-flight demon
in a rush-hour car
all bittered-in like a winter lemon.
Yet and still
        no matter how fast they go,
in a little while they will get
        real slow.

Want to know why?
Want to know why?
'Cause when they cross that bridge,
when they cross that bridge,
on that ridge,
    they are going to see something crouched
up there, lolled up there
to give anybody a scare.
    It will raise their hair.
        Brave or not.
It will raise their natural hair.
See,
    that is where they will meet the lion.
        Green, green lion.
        Fierce.
            Mighty.
                Proud.
        Fierce.
            Smirky.
                Vain.

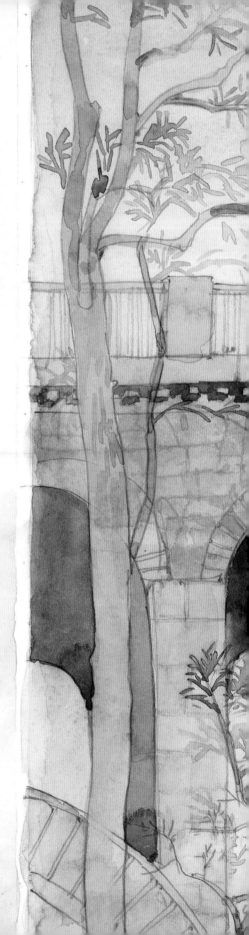

Right on the ridge like a crown. Bold!
Crouched above the city lane.
Green.
Arrogant.
Stern.
Stolid.
Haughty.
Snide.
They think that it will roar out loud.
Its head is higher than gold.
Its jaws are declarative and wide.
You see a mane
and, next, one paw
and then another
And…O Brother!

If you cannot run you are done!
We be's moving!
        We trample the street
        like pounding grain,
        first, two feet up
                and down again
        with courage shattering
        like a summer windowpane.
We be

        a-movering
        a-movering
        a-movering,
                and no ark
        rock
                the way we shock
        the shrubbery
                past the Joggers' Lot.

And sometime we just pass
out on the grass
    and hide and peep
  or act like we have fell asleep.
But it still there.

Its dome of a head supercilious
in the air.
Its countenance still seem to say:
"I am czar. I am here.
And I am not going anywhere."
The look of that kingly beast
with that scowl turned
southeast!
That full imperious stare,
that full disdainful head
of imperturbable
hair.

We stroll back slow
       and lean on the wall—
         prowlin'
         growlin'
         howlin'
R   R   R   R   R
        and laughin' real low….
The bus was late.
The fog is gone.
The lion is clear
    and all alone.
        Just a lion
    and made of stone.
            Stone.
            Stone!

A stone cat
    perched up snooty like that,
    with paws, claws, jaws.
A stone cat
    perched up snooty like that.

We be's looking,
        Checking it out.
        Checking it in.
We walks backward
        and close to, again.
It got a chin
without a grin.
It got an eye
which cannot spy.
It got feet
which cannot cross the street.
It got lips
that do not make sips.
It got a mouth
        hard in stone.
It cannot eat meat
        or chew a bone.

But it get so late
that we leave it—
        'cause the bus—
        the bus has gone.
        The driver came and
        she would not wait—
        and the weather is colder
        than a roller skate.
Still, we went
        and we have seen.
        It is there.
        It is there.

This is not made up.
Would I tell a tale to you?
Have I not better
        things to do?
Right in the city
        in a certain place
a beast is crouched
        with a scowl on its face.
        and it's a lion
                a lion
                a lion

R— lion
    R— lion
        R— lion
The greeniest lion
    you ever could meet,
    reigning right on Zion Street.

R— R— R—R
Lion.